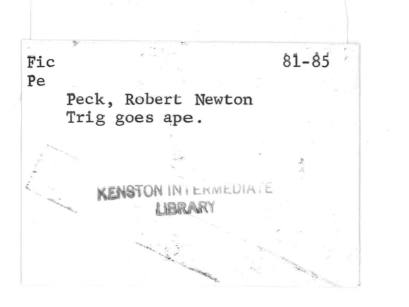

Books by Robert Newton Peck

A Day No Pigs Would Die
Path of Hunters
Millie's Boy
Soup
Fawn
Wild Cat
Bee Tree (poems)
Soup and Me
Hamilton
Hang for Treason
Rabbits and Redcoats
King of Kazoo (a musical)
Trig
Last Sunday
The King's Iron
Patooie
Soup for President
Eagle Fur
Trig Sees Red
Basket Case
Hub
Mr. Little
Clunie
Soup's Drum
Justice Lion
Secrets of Successful Fiction
Trig Goes Ape

TRIG
GOES
APE

TRIG GOES APE

BY
ROBERT NEWTON PECK

Illustrated by Pamela Johnson

Little, Brown and Company
BOSTON   TORONTO

FIRST EDITION

Library of Congress Cataloging in Publication Data

Peck, Robert Newton.
  Trig goes ape.

SUMMARY: Trig gets in on an uproarious melee when
Buck Fargo's Wild Ape and Monkey Show comes to town.
  [1. Humorous stories]   I. Johnson, Pamela.
II. Title.
PZ7.P339Ts   [Fic]   80-17066
ISBN 0-316-57657-9

HAL
*Published simultaneously in Canada
by Little, Brown & Company (Canada) Limited*

PRINTED IN THE UNITED STATES OF AMERICA

To Elizabeth

TRIG GOES APE

1

"GO," I SAID.

Bud Griffin and I watched as Skip Warner climbed on Mr. Goucher's hayrake and then jumped up and sat on the metal seat. That was the signal for Bud and me to start counting. Out loud.

"One . . . two . . . three . . ."

"Yaaahhh!" hollered Skip. Off he hopped.

It sure was a hot old day; near to noon, and not a cloud in the sky. So I knew how hot that iron saddle would be. Even though there were holes in it. Nobody very sensitive could sit on that boiling metal for much longer than one quick yelp.

Skip bounced up and down.

"Okay," I said to Bud, "it's *your* turn."

Bud didn't seem too eager to try and beat Skip's three-second record. He looked at Skip, who was holding both hands to his butt and dancing around like crazy.

I turned to Bud. "Well, you want to beat Skip's record, don't you? Whoever sits on the seat for the longest time gets to shoot my machine gun at Evelyn."

"Don't do it," warned Skip. "It burns like unholy Hannah."

"I'm tougher than you are," Bud told him.

3

"Maybe," I said. "And maybe not. After all, old Skip sat the hotseat until the count of three. Looks like he's the winner. So far."

Bud looked at the hayrake seat and then back to me. "Trig, how come *you* aren't going to try it? Or are ya?"

"I'm a girl," I said. "And we females aren't supposed to act tough like you guys." I chuckled to myself. "Well, are you tough or tender?"

"I'm real tough," said Bud.

Skip smiled. "Yeah?"

"Get ready," I told Bud, "and as soon as your fanny hits the saddle, Skip and I will start to count. We'll see how gutsy you be."

"Okay, I'm ready."

"Go!"

Bud planted his pants into the seat. We counted. "One . . . two . . . three . . ."

"Aaaahhhhh!!!"

I said, "Hot, isn't it?" to Bud, right after he'd jumped off and was rolling around Mr. Goucher's hayfield. Nothing, my father always said, ever gets hotter than the metal seat of a noonday hayrake. He called it the Devil's Throne.

Bud ran over and splashed down right beside Skip, who was now sitting in a rain puddle, cooling off his personal places that had melted the most.

"Who won, Trig?" Skip asked.

Sure was funny to see those two boys sitting in that little old puddle. I sort of thought there was mud on the bottom. Then, as the two of them stood up, I saw that I'd guessed right.

"Come on, Trig, tell us who's the winner."

4

"A tie," I told them, watching the two boys scowl. "You might even go so far as to say it was a dead heat."

"How'll we decide?"

I was trying to keep from laughing at them and their wet and muddy pants. "Well," I said, "looks to me as if we ought to give each one of you another turn."

"I quit," said Fat Face.

Seeing as Skip Warner was a whole lot bigger than I was, I was real careful never to say Fat Face out loud. But I sure enjoyed saying it to myself. Skip and Bud had bullied me for some time. But that was before my uncle Fred brought me my gun. I was the only kid around who owned an official Melvin Purvis genuine Junior G-man machine gun. And, when you pulled the trigger, it made the loudest noise since the World War.

Owning such a wonder of a weapon made me, Elizabeth

Trigman, the leader of our gang of Junior G-men. Just thinking about such an awesome responsibility made me hold on to my gun a bit tighter.

"And I quit, too," said Bud.

The pair of them looked more than a mite miserable; so I figured that I might as well cheer 'em up, seeing as burning their britches on the hayrake seat had been entirely my idea.

"Come on," I told them.

"Where to, Trig?"

"We're going over yonder to the meadow to find Evelyn." I broke into a run, knowing that Bud and Skip would follow me, like usual. "Let's go," I yelled over my shoulder. But as the gun was getting heavy, I couldn't make myself run too far. So I pulled up short under the big elm tree just this side of the fence.

Bud and Skip caught up. Neither of those two boys could run as fast as I could, especially when their pants were soaking wet. Yet carrying my machine gun always made me whoa down a bit. Why, I asked myself now, should I tote it when Bud and Skip were so handy, and so willing?

"Got a penny?" I asked.

Skip pulled a wet penny from his pocket. "What for?"

"To flip," I told him. "Okay," I said, "here's how it works. Bud, you're heads."

"And I'm tails," said Skip. Fat Face was a real deep thinker.

"I'll flip the penny," I said. "Now, if it lands heads up, Bud gets to carry my gun. But old Skip here gets to shoot Evelyn."

"What if'n it lands tails?"

I sighed, using the same sort of an exhale that Miss Millerton uses in school whenever Skip or Bud recites about how Admiral Dewey captured Vanilla. Neither one of them could find Vanilla on our school map. I was amazed they could even find the school, in Clodsburg.

I tossed up the penny, not caring which way it came down; because I was thinking about the fun we'd have as soon as we could locate Evelyn's whereabouts.

"Heads!"

I handed my official Melvin Purvis genuine Junior G-man machine gun, the greatest toy gun ever invented, over to Bud Griffin. This gave my aching arms a chance to take a breather, as well as an opportunity to wipe my steamy glasses on the hem of my dress. I didn't like wearing my glasses a whole lot. But it sure beat bumping into things.

"Okay," I said. "We move in."

"But where's Evelyn?"

"Oh, I reckon we'll locate her, seeing she's usual a lot closer than reason."

Carefully, we crept up on the fence. I let Skip and Bud go first, for two reasons. One, so I could see how wet their pants were . . . and two, so neither one of them could see me laugh. Of the two pairs of trousers, Fat Face's seemed to be wetter. That figured, seeing as big old Skip wore pants about three sizes bigger than any other kid. He wasn't just fat in the face.

We crawled under the fence.

"Now," I said to Bud, "you can turn the gun over to Skip, because *he*'s the one who gets first crack at Evelyn."

Skip was smiling. And I was hoping he'd be so happy that he'd forget a certain trick I'd played on him, a minute or so ago.

I'd kept his penny.

2

WE HID IN THE GRASS.

"I don't see hide or hair of Evelyn," said Bud.

Skip said, "Neither don't I."

"Be patient, men," I said. "Evelyn'll be coming along in her own sweet time."

"I wish today was *next* Saturday," said Bud, "instead of *this* Saturday."

"Yeah," said Skip. "Me, too."

I knew what the boys were talking about, and so did every kid in Clodsburg, along with most of the grown-ups, who were just about equal excited. Only one more week to wait and it would be coming to town — the famous Buck Fargo's Wild Ape & Monkey Show.

"I can't wait to see Buck Fargo," said Bud.

Skip Warner agreed that he couldn't wait either.

"And *I* can't wait," I said, "to see the star of Buck Fargo's show. They claim that the main attraction is Gloria the Great Gorilla."

"Are you going?" asked Skip.

"Bet your boots."

Bud said, "So am I. Golly jeepers, I wouldn't miss seeing Buck Fargo's Wild Ape & Monkey Show for all the fish in Finland."

"Same here."

"Trig . . ."

"Yup."

"Do you suppose that Gloria is actual as big as the picture we saw in the weekly newspaper?"

I'd seen Gloria's picture. She sure was big, even though Mama warned me that pictures in advertisements are often a size or two bigger than real life. To me, Gloria the Great Gorilla looked plenty big enough, even a shade bigger than my Aunt Augusta.

"Yup," I said, "I sure aim to see that gorilla."

"So do I."

We waited in the weeds. Bud held my machine gun while Skip and I held our breaths. And right then, sure enough, along came old Evelyn.

Lots of folks in Clodsburg talked about how old Evelyn was, even though nobody ever seemed to know for sure. Agnes Kotch stated that Evelyn was no more than twenty years old. Zack Turner was talking to Papa, one time, and allowed that she was at least twenty-five. And then I heard Miss Beekin having a chat with Reverend Toop, claiming that Evelyn was pushing thirty.

However, just about everybody agreed on one matter: Evelyn was the oldest mule in Clodsburg.

Evelyn didn't see us. But we looked at her. She was about as gray as old whiskers, all over, and people in town said that if any living thing was as mean as Old Man Goucher, it had to be Mr. Goucher's mule, Evelyn. She'd kicked half the town.

"Elizabeth," my mother always was saying, usual close to three times a morning, "whatever you do, don't you *dare* go near Mr. Goucher's pasture where he keeps that mean old mule."

"No," I always answered, "I sure enough won't."

Yet here I was, crouching in the tall weeds, alongside of Bud Griffin and Skip Warner, who had become my two closest pals. They weren't the kind of boys that would volunteer to hang around and play with a girl. But I wasn't just *any* girl. *I* had a machine gun.

"Steady," I said to Fat Face.

I didn't want Skip to pull the trigger until dear old Evelyn came closer. Because that would spoil our fun.

"Now?" whispered Skip.

"Not yet," said Bud Griffin.

"Yeah," I said softly. "Wait until she comes real handy."

On came Evelyn. I wondered if she was deaf, or a bit hard of hearing. Either way, she sure didn't seem to take notice of the three of *us*.

"Is it cocked?" asked Skip.

Darn it! I knew there was a step that we'd somehow overlooked. We'd forgot to pull back the cocking lever and ready the gun.

"Okay," I said, "let's cock her back. Real easy."

One of the reasons I sort of liked to pal around with Skip Warner and Bud Griffin, even though they were boys, was because it wasn't too cinchy for *one* kid to cock an official Melvin Purvis genuine Junior G-man machine gun. You had to be near as muscular as Mr. Purvis to pull back the lever.

Skip held the machine gun. Bud and I pulled. Back came the lever, slow but sure, until the machine gun was at the full-cock position. Click, click, click, click, click. It took about twenty clicks in all. Plus one heck of a lot of tugs for each click, but we did it.

My gun was full ready.

Evelyn, so it seemed, didn't notice. Nor listen. Gosh, maybe she *was* a bit hard of hearing, as all she did was graze on the green meadow grass that covered the pasture.

"Ready?" I whispered to Skip.

He nodded.

As Evelyn moved closer to us, step by step, she seemed some larger than I remembered her. Over my shoulder, behind, I saw the fence. And then I was wishing that the fence was between us and Evelyn. But it wasn't.

I whispered to Skip. "Don't forget to flick up the safety catch with your thumb, or you won't be able to pull the trigger."

"Is this it?"

I nodded. "Yup, that's it."

As Skip released the safety, his pink tongue stuck out the side of his fat face. Skip Warner wasn't famous for brains. He would probably, I thought, have to concentrate just to chew gum.

Evelyn moved closer.

"Now," whispered Bud Griffin.

"Hold it," I told Skip. "Let's wait until old Evelyn is real nearby, and it'll be a whole lot more fun."

I couldn't breathe. And, at the same moment, I noticed that Skip and Bud couldn't either. The only soul in Mr. Goucher's meadow, who was doing any breathing at all, was Evelyn.

She sure was a big mule.

"Ready?" I asked Skip.

He said, "Ready."

"Aim."

"I'm aiming to aim right now."

"Fire!"

Standing up, Skip pointed my machine gun at Evelyn Goucher, held it steady, and yanked back the trigger.

BRAATT-TAT-TAT-TAT-TAT.

Bud Griffin and I both covered our ears. That gun of mine sure created one heck of a bothersome racket. It made both my ears ring. Everybody this side of Clodsburg must have heard it. Well, not quite everybody. To be absolutely accurate about it, you'd have to say that the noise from my machine gun was heard by every ear except two:

Evelyn's.

I thought for sure she'd run away, kicking her hoofs in

the air, and scared skinny. No such luck. Instead, old Evelyn just trotted toward us, looking mean. So right then, I up and figured out that Evelyn didn't use her ears for hearing. But for something else. If she suddenly spotted three kids (with a machine gun) that she didn't like, she'd just lay back her ears, as if getting prepared to either kick or bite.

"Run," I said.

Yet I couldn't move. Neither could Skip or Bud. The three of us just stood there in the high grass inside the fence as old Evelyn galloped in our direction. Closer and closer she came, so nearby that I could count her teeth. Evelyn curled back her lip, opened her jaws (ears back) and bit my Melvin Purvis Junior G-man machine gun.

And ran off with it.

3

MONDAY MORNING CAME.

"Let us all stand up," said Miss Millerton, "and face the flag."

Crossing our right hands over our chests, as we always did at the start of a day in school, we recited the pledge. I knew it by heart, which was why we had to cover up our hearts the way we did. Not all of the pledge made sense. Yet I figured it had to get said if we all were to be good Americans.

"I pledge a legions to the flag," it sounded as if the class were saying, "to the United States of America. And to the ree public for Witch Itstans . . . one nation, in a dirigible, with liberty, injustice for all."

Then we sat down again. Miss Millerton mentioned something about geography, but I couldn't help thinking about Mr. Goucher's mule.

"We can all see," said Miss Millerton, pointing at the big map of the United States, "that when the early pioneers crossed the plains in their covered wagons, it was almost an endless journey. Indians, hardship . . ."

I yawned.

Today was not a day when I'd be too worried about the pioneers. What really fretted me the most was how I'd ever reclaim my gun. My loss had not been reported to Mama or to Papa, as neither one of them would have approved of our climbing over the fence into Mr. Goucher's pasture in order to draw a bead on Evelyn.

Miss Millerton continued to teach.

"Their covered wagons were pulled, of course, by horses, oxen and mules."

Mules?

I just couldn't hear the word *mule* and not almost bust into tears. My beautiful Melvin Purvis Junior G-man machine gun was a goner. I'd never get it back. Certainly not from Evelyn, who had trotted off with it. And surely not from Old Man Goucher.

"Just think," said Miss Millerton, "how many days it would take just to cross the state of Kansas."

"Where exactly is Kansas?" asked a kid.

"Perhaps," said Miss Millerton, "we shall ask someone to walk up here to the map and show us all exactly where Kansas is."

No one wanted to volunteer.

"Elizabeth Trigman," said Miss Millerton, "would you step forward, please, and indicate where Kansas is located?"

Feeling glued to my seat, I was suddenly aware of being the only kid in the room who had not opened up a geography book. Instead, I had been drawing a picture of my missing machine gun.

"Yes'm," I said.

It sure was a far trek from my seat all the way up to the front of the room and to the big map of the United States. I knew where Vermont was. We all lived here. Kansas, however, could have been anywhere south of the North Pole. Most places were. Nearing the map, I couldn't spot Kansas, even though I squinted at all the states along the Atlantic Ocean.

"Let's see now," I said, my fingers crawling up through Florida and Georgia, "as I recall, after studying my geography lesson, good old Kansas ought to be . . . just . . . about . . ."

I spotted Alabama.

"*Here*," I said. "No, that's Alabama."

Miss Millerton slowly tapped the toe of her shoe.

Scanning the map, I saw Delaware, Maryland, Virginia . . . Wow, we sure had united a whole mess of states. And with all that land to go around, why had they hidden Kansas? Better yet, *where?*

"Up there," I stretched upward on tippy-toe, "is the state of Ohio, just under that lake. And sure enough, there's Kentucky."

"Elizabeth, you were requested, I believe, not to point out all forty-eight states, but to locate just one."

"Yes'm." My mind was still in a daze.

"Have you forgotten which one?"

"Evelyn," I said.

Miss Millerton's eyebrows rose. "Evelyn?"

Over my shoulder, I saw the faces of Bud Griffin and Skip Warner, and both boys were laughing enough to split a gut.

"Sorry," I said.

"I don't recall," said Miss Millerton, "that *Evelyn* has yet been admitted to the Union."

"No," I said, "I don't guess she has."

"Elizabeth, while the rest of us had opened our geography books, what, may I ask, were *you* doing?"

"Drawing."

"You were drawing?"

"Yes'm."

"And you were drawing someone named Evelyn?"

I shook my head.

"Is this Evelyn a friend of yours?"

Darn it! I wanted to cry. No, I was thinking, that doggone old Evelyn was no friend of mine. Worse yet, she ran off with my prize possession.

"No, Miss Millerton."

"Then perhaps you'll forget about Evelyn and do what I asked you to do. Point out Kansas."

Closing my eyes, I charged at the map, hoping I wouldn't land my finger on Mexico. It sort of reminded me of a game we'd played at Al Cuseo's birthday party, a year

back. It was called Pin the Tail on the Donkey. Or was it a mule? Doggone it, everything that was happening today reminded me of old Evelyn.

With both my eyes shut tight, I sort of stumbled toward the map, my hand reaching out and making circles. *Where would I pin the tail?*

My finger hit the map.

The whole class started to clap their hands. But I didn't dare open my eyes. Where, I wondered, had I pinned the tail? I wanted to look up at the map, especially the spot that was under my fingertip. Well, at least the applause I heard was a good sign.

Looking up, I saw Oklahoma.

"Shucks," I said. "Guess I missed."

Then I looked again. Oklahoma was *below* my hand. Just north of it was where my finger was resting on some letters that probably spelled out a word. Moving my fingertip, I saw a beautiful little black *K.* And to think, all along, I'd figured that Kansas started with a C.

"Bull's-eye!" I whispered.

There they were, six little black letters that spelled out K-A-N-S-A-S.

I was home free! I'd won the prize. Pinned the tail on the mule. No, the donkey. I wasn't going to think about Evelyn anymore. Or about Al Cuseo's birthday party. Or my gun. Smiling, I looked at Miss Millerton. "That's it," I told her. "Where I'm touching is Kansas."

"Are you sure it's not Oregon?"

"Yes'm, I'm dead sure. And I guess it was just a hunk of dumb luck that I found it, Miss Millerton. I wasn't paying too much attention to the pioneers."

"Oh really?"

"Yes'm. And to tell you the straight of it, I don't guess I was tight sure of just where Kansas was."

"I understand," said Miss Millerton. She smiled at me and I felt worse than if I'd a got a whack from her ruler.

"Thanks," I said.

"You may return to your seat, Elizabeth, and also return to your geography book."

I sat down.

"This week," said Miss Millerton, "may prove to be difficult as far as concentration is concerned. We are *all* excited, as I am myself, about Buck Fargo's coming to town."

We all agreed on that.

"Imagine," said Miss Millerton, "a giant gorilla. Gloria is going to be right here in Clodsburg."

4

I STAYED AFTER SCHOOL.

Not because I had to. Miss Millerton didn't *make* me do it or anything like that. I just sort of hung around, after the other kids took off, and emptied the big wicker waste-basket. And while I was working I sneaked another quick peek at the map of the United States, so I'd at least re-member where they'd tucked away Kansas.

"Thank you, Elizabeth."

"You're welcome," I told Miss Millerton. "And I'm right sorry I was rude in school today. You know, when I didn't pay a mind about the pioneers."

"I understand. This is an exciting week in Clodsburg, with the big tent show coming to town, and all."

"Are you going?" I asked.

"Of course. Not many souls in this town will want to miss a chance to see Gloria."

"No," I said, "I don't guess they will."

"And are *you* going?"

I nodded. "Yes'm. You bet your sweet life I am. I wouldn't miss seeing old Buck Fargo if you gave me all of Kansas."

Miss Millerton smiled. She had a right pretty grin, and I sure wanted to look like her when I grew up.

I sighed. "I'm glad *I* don't live in Kansas."

"And why is that?"

"Well," I said, "it's so far away."

"Is that the only reason?"

"No. Because if I lived away off in Kansas, instead of here in Vermont, I wouldn't have you for a teacher."

That made Miss Millerton laugh. She said, "I'm sure that the schools in Kansas have their own share of good teachers."

"Maybe. But they're all not you."

"Thank you, Elizabeth. I guess everyone enjoys receiving a compliment now and again. Teachers really are human, you know."

"What's it like to be a teacher?"

"Oh, I suppose it's a bit like being . . . a pioneer."

"I never thought of that."

"Well, it is. You see, Elizabeth, the pioneers had to go without and face wild creatures. Just to survive. And, here in the schoolroom, I have my own little pack of wild creatures."

"And teach us to get civilized."

Miss Millerton nodded.

"But we wouldn't hurt you. We don't scratch or bite or things like that."

"No, but students can hurt a teacher's feelings."

"How so?"

"Sometimes, if I'm trying to instruct the class about geography, and the pioneers, there can be one child who draws guns and doesn't pay attention to the lesson."

I looked down at my feet.

"But, to make up for it, every so often I get the chance

to teach a little girl like you, who stays and empties the wastebasket. Without being asked."

"I wanted to."

"Yes, you did. And I welcome the fact that you felt sorry about drawing during geography. So I guess I'm glad I'm a pioneer. Really glad."

"A pioneer?"

"Of course. Every child's mind is a wilderness. And education is a very long and tedious journey, as in a covered wagon. My job is that of a wagon master, I suppose, to see that all my little wagons move along. One day at a time along the trail."

"I wonder what the end of the trail is."

"We all wonder that, Elizabeth. At least I can see to it, as *your* wagon master, that all the wagons follow along in line. And that no one wagon falls too far behind."

"Okay."

"You don't seem to be yourself today."

I took a deep breath. "No, I don't guess I am."

"Any problem?"

Right then I was thinking about my gun, and wondering if I'd lost it forever. Where had old Evelyn taken it? I just *had* to get it back.

"Yes'm."

"Perhaps I can help."

"It's my gun."

"You want to bring it to school again, I suppose." Miss Millerton covered her ears. "My, but that was one noisy toy."

"I would if I could. But I can't."

"Why not?"

"Because it's gone. I don't own a machine gun anymore. It's just plain gone forever."

Miss Millerton looked concerned. "You lost it?"

"Not quite. I know where it's at. No, that's not right either. Leastwise, let's say I know who's got it and maybe won't ever give it up."

"Who?"

"Evelyn."

Miss Millerton's face made a mild frown. "Ah, the mysterious Evelyn that you mentioned in geography today."

"Yes'm."

"Does she live near you?"

"Real near. You might say *too* near."

"Please tell me Evelyn's full name."

"Evelyn Goucher."

"Did you say *Goucher?*"

"Yes'm."

All of a sudden, Miss Millerton threw back her head, laughing as if she couldn't nudge herself to ever quit. Wiping her eyes with a clean white hanky, she finally stopped.

"You mean that old mule."

"Yes'm. Skip and Bud and I weren't going to be mean, or anything like that. All we were fixing to do was shoot Evelyn, and put a spook to her, so she'd run."

"And poor old Evelyn grabbed your gun."

I nodded my head. "And she just plain ran off, down the meadow, and headed for Mr. Goucher's barn, I reckon."

Miss Millerton sighed. "Elizabeth, I think you have a problem."

"I certain do."

"Mr. Goucher is a rather elderly gentleman who perhaps doesn't quite understand children. I believe he lives alone."

"No," I said. "He's got chickens and Evelyn."

"Plus a machine gun."

"Mine."

"Ah, and if you go to Mr. Goucher to ask for your gun, he may inquire how his mule got the gun in the first place."

"I could make up a lie."

"Yes, you could. If a lie to old Mr. Goucher is what you really wish to tell."

"No," I said. "Lies are dirty."

"Right," said Miss Millerton. She slapped her desk gently with her hand. "And the truth is clean as a cat's mouth."

"What'll I do?"

"Elizabeth, if I were you, I'd do this. First off, I'd locate the exact whereabouts of your gun. Because it *is* possible that Mr. Goucher doesn't have it. And maybe Evelyn doesn't either."

"Okay," I said.

"Do the other children still call you Trig?"

"Yes'm."

But if I lose my gun, I was thinking, maybe I'd have to go back to being Elizabeth all the time. I sure didn't warm up to that idea.

"See you tomorrow, Trig."

"Miss Millerton . . ."

"Yes?"

"You'd a made a right good pioneer."

5

"HEY, YOU KIDS! BEAT IT."

It was Thursday, after school. A beautiful and sunny afternoon in late May. Skip, Bud and I were hanging around the Clodsburg ball park watching all the preparation. I didn't think we were in the way or anything. But our mayor seemed to think otherwise.

"You kids'll get hurt if you get under foot," said Mayor Swagg. "Or dip into mischief."

"No we won't," I said. "Honest."

"Yes you will," said Marvin Fillput. "We have to spruce up the ball park so's it'll be ready for the Buck Fargo Show, on Saturday."

Just about everything worth attending in Clodsburg took place in our town ball park. Church picnics, the Volunteer Fireman's Parade, plus an assortment of religious revivals, political rallies, and holiday outings.

"Where do we set up the seats?" Marvin asked our mayor.

Mr. Fillput was standing behind Orrin Dillard's pickup truck, which was loaded with folded-up chairs. Each chair was marked as property of the Goodrest Funeral Parlor.

"On the ground," said Mayor Swagg. "Where else

would you put a chair . . . up in a tree?"

"Sure," said Marvin, "but in what kind of a formation? In rows, or in circles?"

"Both," said Mayor Swagg.

"Okay."

"Where's the chicken wire?"

"Feldon's to bring it over right soon," said Mr. Fillput. "Fact is, he ought to be here by now. Said he had to stop off at his brother's. But he'll be along right sudden."

"Good," said the mayor.

"What do we use the chicken wire for?"

Mayor Swagg mopped his chubby face. "For a *fence*, Marvin. After all, I'm responsible for the safety of our citizens. We can't have gorillas and apes running all over Clodsburg, can we?"

"Nope," said Marvin Fillput. "I s'pose not."

"Then, soon as Feldon gets here, best we get started to make the place secure."

"Where's the wire go?"

Mayor Swagg unfolded a large piece of paper he had in his pocket. I crowded close to get a better look-see.

"My plan," said the mayor, "is to enclose a sort of arena, the way Mr. Buck Fargo's instructions say to do."

Feldon Jessup arrived. Several bales of chicken wire were roped to the top of his Ford, but a few others had tumbled off, and were dragging in the dust. I never dreamed there was so much chicken-wire fence in Clodsburg. Mr. Jessup's car was practically invisible. It looked like a giant scouring pad.

The car stopped.

"I brung the chicken wire," said Feldon.

Mayor Swagg scowled. "So I see."

"Where's it go?"

"Around the chairs." Mayor Swagg turned to Mr. Fillput. "Now then, how about all the posts? A wire fence won't stand up by its lonesome."

"Herb's supposed to handle that."

"Well, where is he?"

"Doc Ellerby's."

"How come?"

"Claims he got the gout. Sore foot. All swelled up. Herb called me up on the contraption to say he'd be late, on account he can't pull a boot on over his foot."

"It's his *right* foot, too," said Feldon.

"What difference does it make?" asked the mayor.

"Well, you know he sort of rebuilt his Dodge."

"So what?"

"Herb got mixed up putting it back together, and his gas pedal ended up over on the left, with the brake on the right."

"Must be a devil to drive."

"No," said Feldon, "not if you remember one important thing that you always have to do first. Herb does it."

"And what's that?"

"Soon as Herb slides in behind the wheel, he crosses his legs. That way, his *left* foot's on the brake, like usual. And his *right* foot pumps the gas."

Just as Feldon Jessup was completing his explanation of how Mr. Lester still managed to operate the Dodge, we all heard a noise. It grew louder as it came closer.

"What in Sam Hill is that?" asked the mayor.

28

"Oh," said Feldon, "that ain't Sam Hill—it's Herb."

Sure enough, into the Clodsburg ball park (at top speed) roared a Dodge, loaded with fence posts and with Mr. Herb Lester at the controls. Or rather, at the out-of-controls. He was yelling at us, waving his arm out the car window, motioning us all to get out of his way.

He hollered, "I can't stop!"

The Dodge plowed over home plate and headed for first base, knocking over a stack of Goodrest folding furniture.

"Doc put . . . bandage on my . . . foot," yelled Mr. Lester, "Must have . . . gas pedal stuck in the . . . wrapping."

"Told ya so," said Feldon. "It's his *right*. Now if it was his *left* foot . . ."

As the runaway Dodge rounded third base, several fence posts hurtled through the air, some becoming entangled in the chicken wire that seemed to have gotten unrolled all over the ball field.

Mayor Swagg ran for the pitcher's mound, dropping his enormous sheets of paper that seemed to be his plan for the ball park.

"Somebody *do* something!" he yowled.

Feldon Jessup said, "Okay," and started to unload the rest of the chicken wire, tugging at one loose end of a wayward bale. Back it stretched. Around the bases raced the Dodge, and into the length of wire mesh that Mr. Jessup was holding.

I never knew that Feldon Jessup could fly. Yet up in the air he shot, still holding onto the wire, and landed in the silvery nest of chicken wire that covered his Ford. Mayor Swagg, Bud, Skip and Mr. Fillput all watched from our safety island, the pitcher's mound.

"Key," I said.

"Be calm, everyone," said Mayor Swagg. "I'm right here and I'll take care of you children." For some strange reason, the mayor reached out to hug Mr. Fillput. Both of their faces turned pale.

"The key," I said again. "Why doesn't Mr. Lester turn off the key and stop his Dodge?"

Herb Lester finally did stop, with the help of all the chicken wire, several fence posts, and a pile of the folding chairs, many of which looked as if they would never fold, or unfold, again. If they were planning a funeral at the Goodrest Parlor, a good number of the mourners would have to stand.

Color slowly returned to the face of Mayor Swagg, who then said, "Okay, you kids. Best you keep out of the way while we ready the field."

"Why?" I asked.

"Because we *men* have work to do."

6

Deer Mr. Purvis,

Like I wrote to you in my last leter witch you can spot real eazy becuz it had lots of ink blots on it my name is Elizabeth Trigman and my pals call me Trig for short on a count of I am a Junyer G-man and Melvin Purvis is our leader so maybee you can help us solv a crime when Evelyn stool my machine gun and I want it back befor Gloria and the rest of the gurillers get to Clodsburg witch aut to be near as funny as watching Feldon Jessup fly becuz of the way that Herb Laster sits crosslegged in his Dodge after Doc bandaged up his left foot that caught the gowt and smashed the chairs they burrowed from Mr. Goodrest the day that Marvin Fillput hugged our ~~mayor~~ mare on the pitcher mound becuz Mr. Lester didn't turn off the key.

Your freind,
Trig

P.S. His brake is on the right. The other side is gas.

I sealed my letter to Melvin Purvis.

He works for the federal government, which I guess is why folks call him a G-man. Mr. Purvis is the head one. You can hardly listen to the radio, or read a newspaper, without the name of Melvin Purvis cropping up.

It was Friday morning. One more day until Buck Fargo's Wild Ape & Monkey Show arrived in town. I had a hunch that all of Clodsburg was near excited as I was. Mr. Buck Fargo and Gloria the Great Gorilla just about filled up most of the local conversation.

"Hurry and finish your breakfast, Elizabeth."

"I will, Mama."

Only seventy more.

I sighed. Seventy more Soppie box tops and I'd be able to send away to Battle Creek, Michigan, and get an official Melvin Purvis Junior G-man Detective Kit.

"You'll be late for school."

Looking down into my cereal bowl, I counted the soppy, milk-soaked flakes of Soppies. I was usual partial to food. Trouble was, I sure was becoming doggone sick of gulping Soppies every morning. Sometimes, when my mother wasn't looking, I took the box outside and tried to feed Soppies to Mortimer, our boar hog. But old Mortimer doesn't like them either. Nor does our tomcat, Romeo.

"Eat, Elizabeth, *eat*."

I ate.

Closing my eyes, I began to spoon the remaining half a ton of Soppies into my mouth . . . and tried to think about Melvin Purvis.

Melvin's photo was on the back side of the Soppie box. Bright as sunup. Smiling, and saying, "Hi, Kids! I start

33

every morning with a heaping bowlful of Soppie flakes, with plenty of milk or cream, sugar, and fruit. And that's how all my Junior G-men get their energy for a bang-bang day."

Mortimer, Romeo and Elizabeth Trigman were not too interested in having a bang-bang day, or in eating even one more Soppie. There lay the wet flakes, helplessly sinking into the milky mire of my bowl. They just wouldn't go away.

Mama had come to the conclusion that the only thing about Soppies that ever disappeared right away quick was the box top.

Seventy more!

Gosh, I'd be an old woman of twenty or thirty before I could send away for my very own official Melvin Purvis Junior G-man Detective Kit. It was sort of a shame that Skip Warner and Bud Griffin and I couldn't capture all the desperate criminals, and make *them* eat Soppies. At gun-point.

That's what the wardens ought to do, I was thinking. Serve up Soppies in all the prisons instead of bread and water.

"Please hurry, Elizabeth."

Holding my nose, I began to shovel Soppie after Soppie down my gagging throat. Romeo looked up at me and sort of smiled. Our cat sure had it lucky. He got to eat mice.

My churning stomach now sloshing with the best of Battle Creek, I kissed Mama and bolted out the kitchen door, aiming for school and maybe more of Kansas.

One more day.

I trotted, on account it was too pretty a Vermont morning to just walk through. A robin trilled. Looking up, I saw him in one of our pasture elms, with a twig in his bill. Nesting. Soon there'd be a clutch of light-blue eggs, and then babies.

"Morning," I called up to the robin.

It all made me wonder if someday I'd get married and raise up a batch of kids, a litter of new Trigmans. Hold it! I forgot about the fact that when I get wed I won't be a Trigman any longer. Well, one thing certain, I sure didn't aim to become Mrs. Bud Griffin . . . or Mrs. Fat Face. I also figured that neither one of them would be too disappointed.

Skip and Bud were okay, for pals. Leastwise, they always let me be boss. Owning an official Melvin Purvis genuine Junior G-man machine gun sure packed a passel of . . . *prestige?* Miss Millerton taught us that word in school. I liked her a whole lot, even if she was a teacher.

Nobody's perfect.

Passing the Goucher place, I slowed my pace a bit. To take a look-see. Sure enough, there was Evelyn.

She was some distance away, walking through some

sassafras trees that grew alongside Alf's Crick. All I saw was a gray shape, moving right slowly, braiding herself in and out among the scrub trees.

"Evelyn?"

For some reason I called to her, even though I was smart enough to know, by this stage of the game, that old Evelyn's hearing wasn't what it used to be.

I yelled. "Evelyn!"

Just wasting my breath. If she heard me at all, that old gray mule never let on.

"Evelyn Goucher!"

Some folks claim that animals don't have a last name, a family name, the same way people do. Well, not all people have a last name. One man in Clodsburg didn't — old Woodchuck.

Or if he had a last name, there sure wasn't a soul around town that knew it. Woodchuck lived uproad from us, away off in the hills, in an old black tar-paper shanty. He was a recluse, but I thought that if he ever got married he'd have to change his name to Chuck Wood. After all, not too many gals would cotton up to becoming Mrs. Woodchuck.

I laughed.

Miss Millerton read us a story, in school, only last week. She said it was a comedy written by some author guy that won a Pullet Surprise. So I wondered if the author kept chickens. Or beef? Because the story was about a boy who wanted to grow up to be a cook, and his name was Chuck Roast.

I heard a noise. A bray.

Only a mule can hee-haw like a mule. Or laugh like one.

Looking back, I saw Evelyn, who had come up to the fence that ran south of the Goucher place in the direction of town. Evelyn brayed again. A laugh. And then I saw what was so funny to her and so tragic to me.

In Evelyn's mouth was my gun.

7

"GOOD NEWS," SAID MISS MILLERTON.

She was smiling at all of us, so I could tell by the expression on her face that she herself was pleased about what she was fixing to spring on us.

"As today is Friday," she went on to explain, "I shall dismiss you all at noon."

We all cheered. "Hooray!"

"However, we will *all* study extra hard this morning. Is that a fair bargain?"

"Yes'm," we agreed in unison.

"As we all brought our lunches," she said, "we can perhaps have ourselves an outdoor picnic, at noon, if that sounds agreeable."

We all nodded.

"And then, right after our picnic, I have a special treat for the entire class."

"What is it?"

"A surprise. I won't tell you what it is . . ."

We groaned.

"Here now," said Miss Millerton, "there will *not* be any complaining, because this is a special day. So all I want to see on your faces this morning are *smiles*."

I smiled, and so did every kid in the room.

The morning dragged by. I kept looking at the clock, wishing that I could reach up and spin the hands around to point at noon. Straight up.

We ate our picnic outdoors. A breeze stirred up some of the sandwich papers. Miss Millerton insisted that we fetch, collect, and discard them into the trash barrel. Vermont, she always told us, was the most picturesque place in the whole United States to live in, so best we keep Clodsburg looking smarter than Sunday.

Even the birds helped out. A flock of sparrows flew over and combed out a few leftover crumbs from the grass.

"What about the surprise, Miss Millerton?"

Lifting up the little clock that she always wore pinned on her dress, Miss Millerton nodded. That was a good sign.

"I guess it's high time we were on our way," she said.

"Are we going someplace?"

"Indeed we are."

"Where to?"

"Well," said Miss Millerton, "I thought we all might enjoy a casual stroll down to the railroad station, and meet the afternoon train."

"Wow."

There wasn't a single kid in town that needed further explanation. I sure knew who was arriving:

Buck Fargo!

The famous Buck Fargo's Wild Ape & Monkey Show was due into Clodsburg, but I hadn't thought of meeting the train. Just the idea of playing a part in Mr. Fargo's reception almost made me forget that Evelyn still had my machine gun.

"Let's go," yelled Bud Griffin.

Perhaps a leisurely stroll from the schoolhouse down to the railroad station was what Miss Millerton had in mind. However, what she was suddenly a part of was a footrace. Skip was pulling one of her hands and Bud was yanking the other, while I sort of nudged her from behind. It wasn't much of a stroll. And the closer we came to the railroad station, the more people I began to hear.

When we arrived I saw most every citizen we had in town.

Our town band, the Clodsburg Trombone Assembly, seemed to be all present and accounted for, standing under the roof of the station platform. They sure looked splendid, all decked out in their pink and silver uniforms.

Mayor Swagg was there, too, wearing a explorer's white pith helmet. From a leather strap that went around his neck hung binoculars.

"Are you sure," the mayor asked Feldon Jessup, "that the chicken wire is properly in place?"

Mr. Jessup nodded.

"Because," our mayor continued, "we certainly can't have apes and monkeys running loose all over Clodsburg, frightening cows and straining their milk."

"No," said Feldon, "I don't suspect we can."

"Is the band all here?"

"Yes, your honor. Except for Vernon."

"Well," snapped the mayor, "where could *he* be?"

"Don't ask me," said Feldon. "The two of us don't speak."

Vernon Jessup was Feldon's brother. That much I already knew. Yet the fact that they were no longer speaking to one another was news to me. Stepping closer, I perked up my ears.

"It's over Florence," said Feldon. "She's loose."

"Who?"

"Florence. My brother took Florence to the State Fair last September. I told Vernon not to take her. Vernon, I said to him, if'n I was you, I wouldn't take Florence along to the fair. I told Vernon, straight out."

Mayor Swagg scowled. "Who the devil is Florence?"

"Huh," said Feldon. "I thought you knew about *her*. Can't take her anywhere. Nerves, if you ask my opinion. Some can take crowds, but not Florence."

"Why not?"

"She throws up. Can't keep a thing down. And don't

you dare to tell me that Vernon didn't know this, previous, because I swear he did."

"That's a shame. Now is Florence a . . ."

"Hen."

"A *what?*"

"Florence is his best layer. White Leghorn. I ought to know, on account I raised her myself. Gave her to Vernon as a gift, years back, when I convinced him that he ought to go back to school and finish the eighth grade."

"Doggone it," said the mayor, "you mean to tell me that instead of being here with his trombone, Vernon Jessup is off somewhere, with — "

"Florence," said Feldon. "And every time she gets loose, she runs into town here, sees all the people, and throws up. That's why we don't speak, Vernon nor I."

"I see."

"Not only that. Vernon's sore about the wire. So I reckon he can't concentrate enough to toot his trombone when all his chickens are loose."

"I thought you said just Florence got loose."

"Oh, I reckon *she* did, too. Along with five hundred others. It's because of the wire."

"The *wire?*"

"Yup. You know, all those wads and wads of chicken wire I brought over to the ball park yesterday."

"Wasn't that all *your* wire?"

"Nope. It was Vernon's. I guess maybe that's how come all his chickens are loose . . . including Florence."

8

"EVERYBODY BACK!" YELLED MAYOR SWAGG.

We all crowded forward to get a better view of the train as she rounded the bend, belching black smoke, and chugged slower and slower into the Clodsburg depot.

It sure was exciting.

Most excited of all were the Clodsburg Trombone Assembly. It seemed that they had forgotten one minor detail, that being to agree on which particular march they would play. Half of them were tooting *Under the Double Eagle* while the remainder seemed to be partial to *There's a Hot Time in the Old Town Tonight.*

Nobody cared.

I'd seen trains before. Usually the passenger cars were of one color, a dark, pea green that looked like spoiled soup. Today's train was an exception. A few were green, up front; yet the railroad cars that followed were all bright red, orange and yellow. BUCK FARGO'S WILD APE & MONKEY SHOW was lettered on each of the special cars, in silver and gold. It was a sight to see. I was afraid my eyes would blink and make me miss some of the spectacle.

And the band played on.

Skip and Bud boosted me up on their shoulders, at my suggestion, so I could view and report what all the rest of the kids were missing. Even the grown-ups were standing on tiptoe. Having seen Mr. Buck Fargo's photograph on posters that had been, for a week, plastered around every telephone pole in Clodsburg, I knew what he looked like. His handsome young face had also festooned the flanks of many a board fence. Along with a mixture of wild apes, monkeys and Gloria.

"There he is!" someone shouted.

"No," another corrected, "that's the mayor."

We waited, breathless, hearts thumping, and with all necks stretched up like geese. And then our patience was at last rewarded, as Mr. Buck Fargo, also in a white pith helmet, appeared at the door of one of the red, orange and yellow railroad cars.

I could have cried.

Never have I prided myself on guessing people's ages,

and Mama had repeatedly instructed me that I was *never* to ask. And, in this one moment, I wasn't even tempted to ask Buck Fargo.

He was at least eighty-five.

Somebody once said that the oldest living resident of Clodsburg was Miss Beekin, who resided in sedate gentility at Miss Ivy Ransom's Boarding House, and whacked a Peeping Tom with her red rubber bathroom plunger. As far as I could see, Mr. Fargo made Miss Beekin look younger than Shirley Temple.

Eager local hands reached forward to assist Mr. Fargo from the railroad car to ramp level. I expected he'd say a few words but all he did was cough.

He was short and bent over. His body was so crooked he could have hid behind a corkscrew.

When I saw two pith helmets meeting, I knew that Mayor Swagg had finally kicked and punched his way through our friendly crowd to place himself at the side of Mr. Fargo, before the town photographer, Mr. Fromage, poofed a picture.

"Florence?"

Turning my head around, yet being careful not to fall off the shoulders of Bud and Skip, I thought I spotted Vernon Jessup, calling his lost hen.

"Welcome to Clodsburg," said Mayor Swagg, who apparently was not talking to Florence but to Mr. Buck Fargo.

The Clodsburg Trombone Assembly honked out another rendition, sparing no wind into their instruments, and no ear.

I don't know how Bud and Skip did it. Yet they did.

Somehow they managed to ooze through the crowd, carrying me forward and close to where our mayor was pumping the hand of Mr. Fargo.

"Well," said Mayor Swagg, "the village ball park is ready and waiting."

Buck Fargo nodded his pith helmet, which seemed to be several sizes too roomy for such a shrunken head. He must have stayed too long in the African sun.

"You'll be amazed, sir," said our mayor, "at the preparations we've made in order to erect an enclosure to meet your specifications."

I didn't know why Mayor Swagg called them *specifications*. Why couldn't he just called them *apes?*

From up in the air, I really couldn't see any of Mr. Fargo's face. Only the top of his white helmet.

Off to one side, half a dozen strangers started to work — men in dirty coveralls with BUCK FARGO printed on their backs. Some of the letters had faded, and one man proudly sported the name of UCK ARGO.

The fancy railroad cars were opened up, and numerous trunks were unloaded. We couldn't see a single ape. Yet there wasn't a nose in Clodsburg that didn't smell every single one. It was worse than I smelled on the evening when I slipped and fell over the fence into Mortimer's pigpen.

Compared to all the apes, our boar Mortimer was half rose.

"Trig," said Bud, "you're getting weighty."

Skip agreed.

This made me scowl a bit. Why, when both Skip and Bud were always so willing to tote around my Melvin

46

Purvis machine gun, weren't they equal anxious to tote *me?*

"Okay," I said. "Put me down."

The men in coveralls that said BUCK FARGO used the railroad baggage carts to haul their cages through town and over to the Clodsburg ball park.

We all followed.

One of the dirty-coveralls fellows looked at all the chicken wire, cuffed back his cap, and said, "Holy cow. I don't believe it."

"You see?" said a smiling Mayor Swagg, who was still wearing his pith helmet and binoculars. "I told you they'd be impressed."

Doris Jessup appeared, smelled a few cages, held her nose, and then told her husband, Feldon, that he'd best get home to milking. Bending over, she peeked into a crack in one of the cages.

"Is that a monkey in there?" she asked me.

"Well," I said, "I don't guess it's Florence."

Several kids were running around the dirt of the ball park, in the area of where second base usual was. One bumped slightly into a post and over it tumbled, pulling yards of chicken wire down with it. We all helped stand the post up again. Our mayor trotted over to pat the dirt neatly with the toe of his shoe.

"Would you believe it?" Mayor Swagg asked one of the show people. "We actually built this arena ourselves, with our own hands and brains."

"I believe it."

After that, Skip and Bud and I were looking about to see if we could spot a glimpse of Buck Fargo. He wasn't around. Upon asking, we were told by Herb Lester that Mr. Fargo had checked in at Miss Ivy Ransom's Boarding House, and was taking a nap. He'd left orders not to be disturbed.

Watching all the make-ready sure was good sport. And I tried not to think about the fact that Evelyn Goucher still had my machine gun. In her teeth and in her possession.

"Yessiree," said Mayor Swagg, who was parading around his perimeter of chicken wire and loose fence posts, "it'll almost be a crying shame, come Sunday, to have to tear all this down."

He stopped to pick up one of the Goodrest Funeral Parlor chairs that had fallen over. Somehow the chair had folded up and was lying on the grass. Mayor Swagg struggled to open it, folded it again, unfolded it, folded it, and gave up in disgust. Several people ran over to assist him when they saw that he had folded his binoculars into the seat.

Once again I heard Vernon Jessup yelling, "Florence?"

9

"DARN IT!" SNORTED MAYOR SWAGG.

It was early Saturday morning. Skip and Bud and I had gotten up earlier than chores and had legged it into town, straight to the ball park.

Our mayor was still wearing his pith helmet but he had added short trousers and knee sox to complete his safari costume. He should have been *in* a zoo, not at one. But it appeared as though matters were not progressing according to his approval. Mayor Swagg was trying to shoo about fifty or sixty white chickens away from the wire enclosure. And even more were coming.

"Doggone it," said the mayor. "Who owns all these infernal hens? Vernon, are those all yours?"

"Yup," said Vernon Jessup. "And I can't find Florence."

"Well, take 'em home, and that's an order. Florence, too. We can't abide all these dang-fool chickens in here."

"I think they miss their wire fence."

Mayor Swagg sighed. "I know, Vernon. I know. Your dumb brother *borrowed* it. But I promise you'll get it all back, soon as the show's over. Okay?"

"Okay," said Vernon.

"But for now, chase these confounded hens of yours

away from the ball park. They could frighten the apes."

"Yeah," agreed Vernon, "I imagine they just might. I s'pose you heard about Boone Shedlocker?"

"No," said the mayor. "What about him?"

"Well, seems though Boone bought himself a whole flock of chickens."

"Is that all?"

"Nope. One night they busted loose."

"And?"

"Seems like all Boone's chickens run into his pasture and frightened his mule, Sheryl, most to death. She run off, and they found her a week later, clear over to Clemsford Corners."

"Is that so?"

"Sure. Now, I can't say for certain that chickens scare a gorilla. But, boy, oh boy, they sure do spook a mule."

Five minutes later, Skip and Bud and I were chasing chickens. As we ran uproad, each of us yelling and screaming, ahead of us were white hens. I sure hoped Vernon was right about Boone Shedlocker's mule.

"Trig," said Bud, "are you sure we know what we're doing?"

"You bet," I told him.

"I never heard about Mr. Shedlocker's mule getting spooked by a flock of runaway hens."

"Come on," I said. "It's our only chance. We can't be Junior G-men without a machine gun, can we?"

"Reckon we can't," said Skip.

"Up ahead," said Bud Griffin. He pointed his arm. "That there is Old Man Goucher's mule pasture."

"Sure enough is," I said.

"They say that Mr. Goucher's got a temper."

"Okay," I said. "But his mule's got a gun. *My* gun. So I'm fixing to get it back."

"Are you certain all these hens will do the trick?"

"Only one way to find out whether or not Boone Shedlocker's story has got a grain of truth to it. And that's to test it out."

Ahead of us, our flock of chickens seemed to be increasing in number.

"Now or never," I said.

We herded about two hundred chickens into the pasture where Evelyn usual was. Evelyn, and my beautiful machine gun. I kept wishing real hard that Vernon Jessup's story about Boone's flock of hens was accurate.

"Shoo!" I shouted.

Under the fence they went, all those white hens, cackling and clucking, flapping around. I wondered which one, if any, was Florence. None of them seemed to be throwing up. Yet they all appeared to be a mite skittery.

Looking up, I saw why.

Coming our way, and at a full gallop, was Evelyn. Her ears were back.

Suddenly, all two hundred of the chickens became hysterical — jumping up, flapping, snowing the air with flurries of white feathers. I hoped they were more eager to fight a mean mule than I was.

"Something's wrong," I said.

"Like what, Trig?"

"Well, the hens are supposed to scare Evelyn. Trouble is, things seem to be working out the other way around."

"Look again," said Skip Warner.

I looked again. Fat Face was right. Maybe old Evelyn's eyesight was as weak as her hearing because she suddenly bolted straight up in the air. It was as if she suddenly *saw* or *heard* the hens, and Evelyn Goucher sure didn't buddy up to a single one. Not one cluck or one feather. Evelyn kicked, bucked, snorted, and then did something even worse.

Evelyn jumped over her fence!

"Now," I said. "Now's our chance."

"You look over by Alf's Crick," said Bud to Skip. "Trig and I will comb the upper meadow and work down your way. We've got to locate Trig's gun."

"Check."

We ran about as fast as I'd ever run before. To be truthful about it, maybe Evelyn was scared of chickens, but I sure was frightened funny by that old gray mule. Evelyn Goucher had a look in her eye that seemed to say how little respect she had for a kid named Elizabeth Trigman. She might come hastening back.

"Trig!"

The voice came from down by Alf's Crick. It was Skip. So old Bud and I ran in his direction. Sure enough, Skip found it.

"Here it is, Trig."

"Wow," I said. "Thanks, Skip. You're a pal. And so help me, I'll never call you Fat Face again. At least not for another week."

Skip looked puzzled. "Fat Face?"

"Forget it," I told him. "Just a slip of the tongue. Skip, how would you like to lug my gun back into town?"

"Boy, would I! Thanks, Trig."

"Shucks," I said. "What are pals for?"

"And then," said Bud Griffin, "I get to carry it all the way home for ya, Trig. Okay?"

"Right," I said. "After all, we Junior G-men gotta stick together. All for one."

"Hey!"

I looked where Skip was pointing, and couldn't believe what I saw. Evelyn was galloping down the road, headed for town.

"I'll be darned," said Bud.

The chickens were all chasing Evelyn.

10

"WON'T IT BE REAL NIFTY, TRIG?"

"Sure will be," I said, "as soon as we can catch our breath from all the running we did."

Skip was winded worse than I was, seeing as he had to carry my official Melvin Purvis genuine Junior G-man machine gun.

"Yeah," said Bud, "I can hardly wait for the show to start."

Looking at the Clodsburg ball park, I could tell at a glance that our day's entertainment was near under way. There seemed to be more chickens than people. Evelyn must have been nearby, but I didn't spot her. Mayor Swagg, still in his short pants and pith helmet, was trying to corner every hen that came close. So far, as I could readily tell, he hadn't caught any. As we came closer, I heard him yelling for somebody, with both lungs.

"Vernon!"

"Right here," said Vernon Jessup, who at last was wearing his band uniform.

"Dang it, I thought I asked you to round up all your infernal hens and shoo 'em back to home."

"I'm trying to, Your Honor. But it's time to form up the band, like you said."

Pulling out a pocket watch, Mayor Swagg checked his timepiece. "The show's about to commence. And we can't ask Mr. Buck Fargo to perform his wild animals in a hen yard. Can we?"

Vernon said, "Reckon we can't. I'll try."

Most of the folding chairs from the Goodrest Funeral Parlor were already occupied by Clodsburg behinds. More people were hurrying to get a seat up front. I saw Edna Ellerby, Doc's portly wife, select a seat, and then sit down. All the way! One thing for sure about folding chairs, they certainly do fold. Edna crashed to the ground in short order and did a bit of folding herself.

"Need a doctor, Edna?" asked Orrin Dillard as he shot a wink in Doc Ellerby's direction. "Too bad we don't have one in town."

Seeing as Orrin's cousin Bert owned the Goodrest Funeral Parlor and all its folding chairs, Doc didn't appear to be all that amused. It took two men, plus about seven or eight kids and a chicken or two, to get Mrs. Ellerby stood up.

And then, when Bert Dillard came over to offer her another chair, she kicked it; and Doc said a word or two that didn't sound too medical.

"Hey, Trig," said Bud Griffin, "here comes the band."

Sure enough, the Clodsburg Trombone Assembly, now complete with missing trombonist Vernon Jessup, entered the ball park in their pink and silver uniforms. Their musical instruments sparkled in the sunshine.

Meanwhile, with the help of the Clodsburg Volunteer Fire Fighters, almost all of the white chickens had been

56

chased away by a fire hose that had been hastily hooked up to the ball park's only hydrant.

I didn't expect it, but Buck Fargo's Wild Ape & Monkey Show also had a band of its own. It sure wasn't much. Yet out they came in green suits, carrying every size and shape of *drum* you could ever imagine.

A man from the show came by and told us to go buy our tickets or he'd see to it that the three of us got tossed into jail, for trespassing. So we each had to cough up a quarter. Grown-ups had to pay fifty cents.

Mr. Fargo's drum band started to beat their drums and tried to make Clodsburg sound like some place in Africa. I was hoping that they might howl out some kind of a war-whoop, like savage cannibals do in Tarzan movies. But the only scream we heard came right after the collapse of Edna Ellerby's second funeral chair.

I thought about suggesting to Mrs. Ellerby that she stay away from all future funerals. A yowl like hers sure could wreck the quiet.

The drums stopped.

Then, as a ringmaster's whistle suddenly sounded, out into the big ring of chicken wire limped the star of the show: Mr. Buck Fargo. He wore a white suit that looked as if it hadn't been washed since Columbus landed, boots, and his white pith helmet.

"Trig," said Bud, "what kind of hat is that?"

I said, "Pith."

"Wash out your mouth," Mrs. Ellerby told me.

Buck Fargo held up a red and yellow megaphone to his mouth and said, "Ladies . . . and gentlemen . . . we take pride in presenting to you, at this time, the one, the only, the original . . . Buck Fargo Wild Ape & Monkey Show!"

Clodsburg applauded. But not too loudly, as it would take more than just a megaphone to impress us and the rigid standards we set for high-class entertainment.

After all, we'd been over to Clemsford Corners last summer, and heard and seen the *Major Bowes' Amateur Hour*. Feldon Jessup's sister, Grace Jessup, won the trophy and a five-dollar cash prize. That was because she could dance and sing *and* play a music instrument. All at the same time. Her dancing was about as graceful as a mule's, and her singing sounded worse than Evelyn's most throaty hee-haw. But not many folks could play a harmonica the way Miss Jessup could — blowing it through her nose.

Folks here in town called her Amazing Grace.

"And now," continued Mr. Fargo, not through his nose

but through his colorful megaphone, "our first act will be performed by our pet monkey . . . the one we named . . . Wrench."

Buck Fargo patiently waited until, one by one, the faces of Clodsburg finally brightened as Monkey Wrench's name at last hit home.

Wrench scampered out into the ring, tossed a ball, jumped through some hoops that had once been circles but were now bent out of shape (worse than Mr. Fargo), and blew a note or two on a tin bugle. He was dressed up in a bellhop costume.

"Trig," said Skip, "what kind of a monkey *is* that?"

"Well," I told him, "in my zoo book, I think they named it a spider monkey. He's got what they call a *utensil* tail."

"What's that?"

"I guess it means they use a spider monkey in a kitchen, to help cook. Mama calls our old black frypan a spider, so I reckon it must be why. And she's always saying, as she gets supper ready, that she's only got one pair of hands."

I figured my mother, like Wrench, sure could have used a utensil tail.

I watched the monkey for a while, then I yawned. For my taste, Wrench wasn't exactly my idea of a talented specification. When, I wondered, would we all get to see Gloria the Great Gorilla?

Two chimps came out and worked a teeter-totter, see-sawing up and down, while we clapped a few times, just to be polite. This outstanding eye-opener was followed by a trio of monkeys, dressed up sort of like Mr. Fargo, who chased a parrot with butterfly nets. The parrot seemed to be missing far more feathers than it had. Finally the bird was captured by one of the nets.

And right then, the many ears of Clodsburg were rewarded when the parrot screeched out a whole sentence of dirty words. Real zingers!

"The show's improving," I said.

11

"THIS SHOW IS A BLASPHEMY."

So spoke Reverend Toop as he stood up to protest the parrot's creative conversation. I wasn't quite sure what "blasphemy" meant. It might have something to do with dynamite.

Mrs. Rixbee, sitting two rows behind Reverend Toop, requested that he sit down. Using the crook of her umbrella handle, she yanked His Reverence back into his seat. It folded.

It was fun to watch Reverend Toop fold up with it, and go down. In church, during his lengthy Sunday sermons, he often warned *us* all about descending.

Bud said, "Ya know, Trig, those chairs from the Goodrest Funeral Parlor sure do add to the celebration."

Fat Face agreed.

"At this time," announced Buck Fargo, "we proudly present, for your viewing and listening pleasure . . . a tomtom solo . . . performed on his very own drums by none other than . . . our very own . . . Professor Milo Fillput."

Oddly enough, no one seemed to notice the professor as he stood up to take a bow. Instead, the eyes of Clodsburg turned to stare at one of our local citizens, Marvin Fillput, who was seated next to Mabel Kimmer. They were holding hands.

If, I began to think as the professor pounded away, you've heard one thump on a worn-out tom-tom, you've heard 'em all. Milo, in my opinion, was hardly more entertaining than Marvin, who hardly could be called a box-office smash. Except maybe to Mabel when I saw them once, out parking behind the old sawmill.

The crowd grew restless. Our coughing and fidgeting alerted Mr. Fargo, who decided it was time either to get out of town or bring on his main attraction.

"Folks," said Buck Fargo through his megaphone, his hoarse old voice giving it all he had, "here comes the act you all have been waiting so patiently to see."

"About time," said Doris Jessup.

"Now," intoned Mr. Fargo, "from the wilds of darkest Africa, right here to . . . to . . ."

"Clemsford Corners," yelled out Norm Gibbard, who was well known as one of Clodsburg's keener wits.

"Right here to Clodsburg Corners," repeated a somewhat confused Mr. Fargo, "we proudly present . . ." He paused. "Hang on to the kiddies, all you parents. There may be a mite of danger in what you are about to witness."

All the mothers dutifully grabbed the arms and ankles of their popsicle-stained young, hauling them closer to the apron of maternal protection. From somewhere in the crowd, I could hear my mother calling out my name: "Elizabeth?"

"In . . . tro . . . ducing," said Mr. Fargo, "one of the most ferocious beasts of the African jungle . . . captured on the very banks of the Zambezi River . . . our feature attraction and main event . . ."

"Bring her out, Buck," yelled Norm Gibbard, "before the both of ya die from old age."

"Gloria, the Great Gorilla!"

I had noticed, yesterday, that one of the cages *was* larger than all the others. And smelled stronger. This was the very cage that the men in the dirty coveralls were now approaching. The cage was even bigger than Charlie Dingo's outhouse.

The rusty old door slowly slipped upward as all our eyes probed the dark interior, anxiously hoping to spy a first look at Gloria. The men prodded with long poles.

Out she came.

"Glory be," said Miss Beekin. "She's *naked!*"

I had not expected to see a naked ape. The monkeys and chimps had all worn little costumes of colored silk and spangles. But not Gloria.

Reverend Toop, for some strange reason, lifted up both hands to cover his eyes.

There didn't seem to be a whole lot of danger, even though it was obvious that Gloria was indeed a full-grown gorilla. Naked or no. Whatever she was, Gloria was also very, very sleepy. And more bored than we were. She lay down in the circle of sawdust, picked her nose, closed her eyes, and slept.

"Boo!" yelled Clodsburg.

Because, after all, fifty cents was fifty cents, and old Gloria didn't appear to offer a whole lot of amusement.

But that was before the next attraction entered the enclosure, to join Gloria and Buck Fargo. No one quite expected the center-ring duet to suddenly become a trio.

"Hey!" yelled Mr. Goucher. "That's my . . ."

He was right. It was Evelyn, and she was terrified. I didn't think that the entire U.S. Army Field Artillery could wake up Gloria the Great Gorilla, but Evelyn Goucher sure did. In one second and with one loud hee-haw.

Now Gloria was terrified, too.

On came Evelyn, and right after her all five hundred of Vernon's white chickens poured into the arena. Ears back, and wild in the eye, Evelyn Goucher was one scared mule.

And even Buck Fargo himself, he who had faced the ferocious fates of wildest and darkest Africa, seemed suddenly to be running around like a scared ninny.

"Holy cow," said Bud. "Trig, isn't this the best show you ever saw?"

"Yup," I said. "Can't beat local talent."

I had to admit that Boone Shedlocker was right. Mules *are* afraid of chickens. But then it appeared that, hysterical though she was, Evelyn was fairly calm and collected compared to Gloria. Was this the first time that Gloria the Great Gorilla had ever seen a chicken? Or had been surrounded by five hundred of them, all cackling? I could see how upset Mr. Vernon Jessup had become. I hoped he could somehow locate his favorite hen.

"Trig," said Skip, "look quick!"

I looked.

No one who wasn't at least half crazy could ever believe what we all saw. I *never* would have guessed that a gorilla could ride a mule. Gloria, encircled by enraged chickens, vaulted up on Evelyn's back.

Evelyn started to buck like a bronco in a Wild West rodeo. That old gorilla hung on tighter than a leech but Evelyn Goucher sure had plenty of kicks left in her.

Mr. Goucher yelled out a "Whoa!"

Mayor Swagg, taking immediate command, shouted an order for somebody to *do* something. But, as it was a hot day, we all froze. At last we were getting our fifty cents' worth.

Evelyn, with Gloria astride her swaying back and clinging like glue, obeyed our mayor's order. She did something. Evelyn kicked over the chicken-wire fence.

Clodsburg jumped to its feet. Women screamed. Men fainted. And five hundred hens flapped around, chasing Gloria and Evelyn into the crowd of five hundred wild-eyed people.

"Catch that mule!" hollered Mayor Swagg. "No, what I mean is, catch the gorilla!"

Doris Jessup grabbed a butterfly net.

12

"PLAY SOMETHING!" Mayor Swagg yelled to our hometown band. "Music can soothe a savage beast. I hope."

The Clodsburg Trombone Assembly acted on command, tooting out a rousing rendition of *Down in Jungle Town*. But it didn't sound too soothing.

Evelyn bucked, but Gloria the Great Gorilla stayed aboard, her big black fingers maintaining a firm grip on Evelyn's mangy mane. Doris Jessup chased both of them with her newfound butterfly net. Feldon Jessup was trying to protect his snarls of chicken wire from further destruction.

Reverend Toop yelled out a prayer.

Our band didn't sound as loud and clear as usual. Then I saw why. Vernon Jessup, trombone and all, had left his fellow musicians and was running around in the sawdust in an effort to recapture all his chickens. He jumped over a specification.

Woodchuck stood up on his Goodrest Funeral Parlor chair and let out one heck of a holler. Evelyn's hoof kicked over a cage. Its door slid open, allowing several chimps to escape. And a monkey was now riding poor old Miss Beekin.

"Help!" she hollered.

Running to assist her, Mrs. Rixbee swung her umbrella like a baseball bat, but missed hitting the monkey. Instead, she bashed Reverend Toop, who mentioned God again.

But no prayer would stop Mrs. Rixbee. Again she swung at the monkey, and didn't miss. She knocked Miss Beekin into Doris Jessup, who spun the handle of her net and cracked poor Woodchuck right smack in the middle of his next yodel.

The umbrella unfolded just as Woodchuck's chair folded. Woodchuck fell, landing on Marvin Fillput, who was just about to kiss Mabel Kimmer. That caused Marvin to stumble forward and, by error, kiss a chimp. Taking a look at Marvin, the chimp wiped its mouth. And spat.

"Evelyn!" screamed Mr. Goucher.

The air above us was almost white because of at least a million chicken feathers swirling around. Mayor Swagg lost his pith helmet trying to climb over the chicken wire. Then his foot got caught in the long silver loop of Vernon Jessup's trombone, which one of the chimps had picked up and was attempting to play. The trombone (or the chimp) made a rather disgusting noise.

Gloria rode Evelyn around and around the sawdust circle. The monkey still rode Miss Beekin.

Our local volunteer firemen couldn't seem to think of anything else to do, so they turned on the big hose. Water gushed out, soaking everyone in town, and the hose, which was acting up like an insane snake, wrapped itself completely around Orrin Dillard. Nobody had bothered to hold the nozzle.

The show was worth at least a quarter.

Right then, I heard a horn toot. Turning around to look, I saw Herb Lester coming full speed in his Fixit Garage Dodge. The one with the gas pedal on the left and the brake on the right. I'd hoped that Mr. Lester's gouty foot was getting better. Perhaps it was, yet he must have forgotten his most important step — to cross his legs before driving.

His old Dodge seemed to have a mind of its own, and wanted to chase chickens, the mule, and Miss Beekin, who was still serving as the mount for a monkey. Mrs. Rixbee and her umbrella continued to whack everybody, even Buck Fargo.

"Trig," said Bud, "there's only one thing to do."

"Yeah," said Skip, "and let's do it."

"Okay," I said. "I guess it's time we Junior G-men took over. So here goes!" I pulled the trigger of my machine gun.

BRATT-TAT-TAT-TAT-TAT.

It worked!

Everybody stopped. Even the Dodge. And the mule, the monkeys, the chimps, the gorilla, plus all the hosed-down folks of Clodsburg, who were now more soaked than Soppies. I wished that Mr. Melvin Purvis could have watched me as I shot off my machine gun.

All was quiet.

Even the chickens stood stiller than stones, except for just one. In the center of the ring of busted chicken wire, one white hen flapped her wings, and clucked three times, as she layed an egg on the sawdust.

And threw up.

Vernon Jessup and his trombone rushed forward. He

was smiling as he rescued her. Happily holding his prize chicken, he walked over to his friends. And then, in the hushed joy that we all shared with him, Vernon said just three words:

"I found Florence."

13

It took an hour to capture all the animals.

Cornering the chickens was the hardest job, and it seemed to me that almost every citizen in town was holding a hen. Except for Reverend Toop, who was holding his battered knee and looking for Miss Beekin with revenge in his eye.

Miss Beekin was found later — she had hidden herself inside one of the monkey cages.

Buck Fargo's Wild Ape & Monkey Show was finally packed and prepared to move on. I heard Buck let out a deep sigh, and then remark to Mayor Swagg, "Clodsburg is one town to remember."

Our mayor smiled. "Gee, thanks. I hope you'll bring back your show next summer."

"We'll be back. But next time around, I shall insist on one small change in the arrangements."

"Oh," said Mayor Swagg, "and what's that going to be?"

"Next summer," said Buck Fargo, "our apes and monkeys will pay a quarter to watch Clodsburg."